PRAISE FOR CANNON THE BROWN BEAR

"As an experienced educator, Kyle McGrath knows that America's children are not learning the important lessons of self-reliance and independence that must be instilled if the next generation is to lead our nation into the future. His original children's book -- complete with lovely illustrations -- reinforces these values and helps children understand that dependency on others doesn't really make us happy. It's taking care of ourselves -- and experiencing the joys of independence -- that build genuine self-esteem and pride. A great and timely message for America's children!"

- Marybeth Hicks, columnist for the The Washington Times and author of Don't Let the Kids Drink the Kool-Aid

"Kyle McGrath has created a wonderful introduction to the value of individual liberty and free enterprise. Any child will enjoy this entertaining and enlightening book - with a wonderful and moral message!"

- Doug Ross, editor and author of DirectorBlue.blogspot.com

"This book has a powerful message children and many adults should learn- Cannon the Brown Bear lost his pride in himself and his dignity when he accepted that people should provide for his food and well being, but he recovered them again when he once more took care of himself, hunting for and eating foods that he really wanted to eat and preparing his den as a proud bear would. And in the process he became healthier and happier. Well done indeed!"

- Jim Gourdie, editor and author of ConservativesOnFire.wordpress.com

Named to the 2014 Mamie Eisenhower Library Project book list as one of the books that the National Federation of Republican Women believe empower and motivate future generations of children.

Copyright © 2013 by Kyle McGrath

Printed by CreateSpace Independent Publishing Platform, a brand of On-Demand Publishing LLC, part of the Amazon group of companies.
Printed in United States of America
First printed 2013
Edition: 3.0

ISBN-13: 978-1483966830
ISBN-10: 1483966836

This is a work of fiction. Names, characters, businesses, places, events and incidents are either the products of the author's imagination or used in a fictitious manner. Any resemblance to actual humans or to actual events is purely coincidental.

Bookstores and Online Retailers - This book is available to purchase and distribute to your customers, both online and offline, through retailers such as Barnes & Noble and to distributors such as Ingram and NACSCORP.

Libraries and Academic Institutions - This book is available to purchase through Baker & Taylor.

Certified Resellers - This book is available to purchase for certified resellers through the wholesale website CreateSpace Direct.

Thank you family and friends for your help and encouragement, especially my wonderful wife who lovingly illustrated this book for me.

Cannon the Brown Bear:
an Illustrated Children's Fable
Written by Kyle McGrath
Illustrated by Michaela McGrath

This is the story of the year when a six year old brown bear named Cannon had his whole life changed.

Cannon was a brown bear who lived in the hills out west. He roamed the forests, munched on tender roots and ripe berries and crunchy nuts, dined on sweet honeycombs he found, and hunted fresh salmon in the streams.

He had to work hard and did not have a lot of free time. But he ate what he wanted and did what he wanted, and so was healthy and happy.

Like other bears, Cannon dug himself a den before winter. With care, he choose the perfect spot in the nearby hills. He found a spot sheltered from the snow. And then he dug a cozy yet large den that would keep him warm through the winter.

Usually he looked forward to another year of hunting, fishing and hiking around the great outdoors. But before Cannon went into hibernation, he had a thought. He thought that life might be easier if only someone provided everything for him. He could do nothing every day, yet still enjoy tasty food and sleep in a nice den.

So Cannon went to sleep that winter dreaming thoughts of free food and a den dug out for him. But he was going to learn that there is no such thing as a free lunch.

The next spring, Cannon woke up from his long sleep with a yawn. He emerged from his den to seek out the first tender yummy roots that spring time brought. But before he got a couple steps, he discovered something.

During the winter, someone had found his den and thoughtfully left out a bucket of food for him. In it were potatoes, eggs and an apple. He did feel hungry after his long sleep, even though he didn't really like that sort of food and the food was a bit rotten. He also felt uncomfortable- he hadn't earned that food. But it was right there.

So Cannon ate all the food. His stomach was a little upset afterwards. And there was now no reason for him to get up and hunt. So he laid back down to nap for a little longer.

3

Cannon woke up some time later. He was a bit stiff and sluggish when he emerged again from his den. He found that the bucket had been refilled with more food. Now it was filled with slimy salmon, tough seeds and stale berries.

Again, he felt a little guilty eating food he had not earned through his hard work. And again, the food wasn't really even that good. But it was right there and he hadn't had to do anything to get it. So he ate it.

As he munched on the food, he did wonder to himself who was refilling the bucket and why they thought he needed their help. After all, he had been getting on decently enough before, although he did have to work hard. Deciding to do a bit of exploring, he set off down the hills into the valley below.

Cannon wandered down from the hills into the valley and found that some buildings had been built in the valley over the winter. A sign on the building had the following written on it- 'Park Service'.

Inside the buildings Cannon noticed many people moving around, all wearing brown pants and grey shirts and tan hats. Those must be park rangers, Cannon thought. And they must have been the ones who had left out the food for him.

Although usually a little cautious around people, he saw a picnic table nearby. He decided to sit down for a bit and rest. To his surprise, he found on the picnic table a hunk of salmon. It was a little stale and he wasn't even hungry, but it was free so he ate it.

With nothing else to do now, he grew bored. He decided to wander back to his den and just go back to napping. But he wasn't really tired, so instead he just laid in his den wondering.

He wondered why he was being given all this free food. He knew that he had done nothing to earn it. And he knew that someone else must have had to do something to get it. After all, he thought, fish don't just jump on to tables. And rotten berries don't just gather in a bucket. And potatoes don't just appear in front of his den.

So Cannon knew that someone else must be putting some work into giving him that food.

Cannon felt a bit uncomfortable at what was happening. But he did like how the food was just there and free to him.

So the next time he got hungry, he decided that he would try the picnic table again. It was easier then spending time and energy hunting. He cautiously approached the buildings and sat down at the picnic table.

He found that the park rangers had indeed left out a bunch of stale berries for him. So he sat down and ate. While he ate them, he thought fondly of the time he had used to spend roaming over the wilderness looking for honey combs, roots, and nuts.

Cannon spent the next several weeks napping and hanging out in his den. Feeling a little bored and with nothing to do, he found himself spending a lot of time listening to the wind in the trees and sunning himself in the spring sun.

He didn't work hard anymore to find food. There was always something waiting for him at the picnic table, set out by the park rangers.

At first he felt guilty about just taking the hand outs. But after a while he got used to that feeling. And then he stopped caring or thinking about how he got the food. He just ate it.

Cannon the Brown Bear soon stopped hunting, fishing or even looking for food. He no longer explored, went for walks in the forests, or hiked over the hills. Every day he would just wander down to the picnic table and wait to be fed.

It was a lazy and boring year for Cannon. He noticed that he was no longer in shape. He began to put on weight. His coat wasn't as shiny and soft as usual. And he was frequently unhappy. But the food hand outs just kept him coming back.

Spring passed, and summer too. Cannon found himself forgetting what the woods looked like. He often day dreamed about hunting and fishing on his own. But he didn't feel like he had any choice- the food just continued to be set out for him.

Winter came, and so Cannon climbed back up the hills to make a den. Panicking a little at the thought of doing some actual work on his own of digging out his den, he slowly climbed the hills. He was soon panting hard, since he was so out of shape. But he was relieved when he discovered that the park rangers had dug out his winter den for him.

The den was a more cramped and leaky than the one he would have dug himself. It was actually pretty uncomfortable.

But Cannon thought that bears who idled away their days couldn't afford to be choosy about their den. After all, he had not dug one himself. So he ignored the poor home that had been given to him and squeezed into it for another winter of hibernation.

Like last winter, he thought about the coming year. He felt bad about taking all that free food. It was below his standards. And he knew that he had time and strength to find his own food and build his own den. Before he feel asleep that winter, he decided that next year he wouldn't beg but would work on his own.

But when spring came and Cannon woke with a yawn, he was hungry. He found himself angrily falling back into his previous habits. Disliking what he was doing, he ambled down from the hills into the valley below to the buildings where the park rangers lived and sat down at the picnic table. He found himself waiting for his handout of food like last year.

But there was no food on the picnic table this time.

Even though he waited for a good while, no one brought him anything. Cannon looked around. He noticed now that the buildings were empty and shut down. There were no more park rangers. He was on his own again.

Scared and anxious, Cannon sat down in the high grasses and thought hard. He knew that if they didn't come and provide him with free stuff, he would be forced to learn all over again how to take care of himself. And that scared him.

After a year off, he didn't really know if he still knew how to hunt or fish or forage any more. And he had indeed forgotten where all the good honeycombs and nuts and berries were. He was afraid that he had even forgotten how to make a den for himself.

Cannon had gotten used to the free handouts and someone doing the hard work for him. He was out of shape and continually tempted to just lie down and nap. But he knew that the park rangers weren't coming back. He would have to work hard again and provide for himself. And so he did just that.

Whatever the reason, Cannon was happy again. He didn't know if it was because he was being productive. Or if it was because he enjoyed exploring and discovering new things. Or maybe because the labor made him healthier and strong. Or perhaps it was just pride in ownership.

Cannon soon found himself enjoying wandering through the forests and finding his own food.

Cannon really enjoyed the food that he found for himself. Now he could compare it to the free handouts that the rangers had given him.

The food he found himself was better than the food he had been given for free. It was more natural, it was the food he really wanted and he valued it more since he had had to work for it.

He even found a fresh and tender root to eat- something that the park rangers had never set out for him.

The den that Cannon dug himself also was even better than the one that the park rangers had made for him the previous winter.

Cannon dug out a den that was cozy and warm and not damp at all. He took great care in its building and preparation, since it was going to be his home for the coming winter.

He was so proud of the den he had made himself. Cannon even decorated the entrance to his den with some artwork.

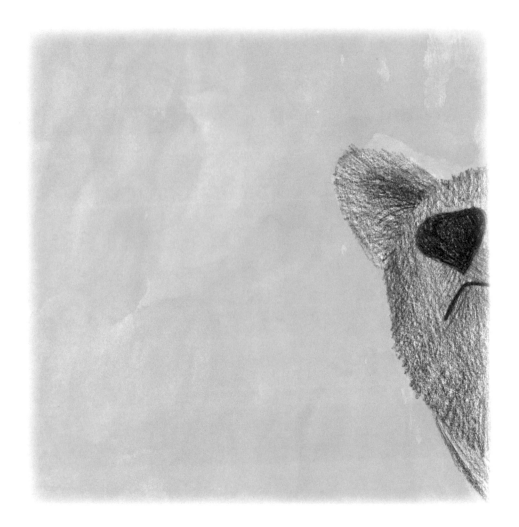

Cannon began to notice that he had much more energy. He certainly was physically stronger. And his mind was clearer, and he could once more think about all those things that free bears think clearly about. The anger, fear, depression, and boredom that had come with being dependent on others began to fade.

Although not every day he was successful finding food, most days he did. And he did it on his own terms relying on himself. This made the honey he found on his successful days that much sweeter.

Cannon felt himself growing in pride, character, courage, and self-reliance. And all this came from simply working and providing on his self and not relying on hand outs from others.

Over that summer, the memory of receiving handouts and living in a boring fog of dependency began to fade away.

Cannon occasionally would think about how much easier it had been when he was given handouts. But he would quickly catch himself and also remember how unhappy and unhealthy he had been.

Cannon had learned his lesson about how wrong it was to be dependent on other people. And about how right it was to work for oneself and to provide for oneself. Cannon now knew that being self-reliant is a good and wonderful character trait to have.

Cannon the Brown Bear had once again become a self-sufficient bear.

He was free from being dependent on others. He was free to make his own destiny. He was free to make his own way in the world. And so he did.

Cannon spent the rest of his days happily roaming the forests, munching on roots and berries and nuts, dining on honeycombs, hunting salmon in the babbling brooks and streams, and sleeping the winters away in a nice den that he would dig himself.

The End

Afterword

The story of Cannon the Brown Bear is a familiar tale about the value of self-reliance. Self-reliance is having trust and confidence in one's own capabilities, judgment, or resources. And this value can help a young child grow in independence and become a stronger person.

But children are not born with the value of self-reliance, but are rather blank slates to be written upon. They must be taught the meaning of value of self-reliance. And then through conversation and stories and games it must be encouraged in them so that they become excited about this value and work to become more self-reliant on their own.

Parents must play an important role in this process. Curriculum in most schools do not teach self-reliance, movies or television shows today rarely encourage it, and many modern day children's books feature characters excited in many values but rarely self-reliance. If parents do not teach and excite this value in their children, then perhaps no one will and children will instead grow up to be dependent.

Children who are not taught the value of self-reliance, or for whom the value is not encouraged and excited, will instead learn and value dependency on others. No longer trusting their own capabilities, judgment, or resources, children will become reliant on others and unable to shape their own future. No parent wants this for their child.

Conveying, cultivating, and encouraging a value like self-reliance is difficult, so this story and the illustrations in it were intended to help in this effort- and also to add a little bit of excitement, humor and wit to the effort.

Theodore Roosevelt once said "If an American is to amount to anything he must rely upon himself, and not upon the State; he must take pride in his own work, instead of sitting idle to envy the luck of others; he must face life with resolute courage, win victory if he can, and accept defeat if he must, without seeking to place on his fellow man a responsibility which is not theirs."

Take inspiration from Cannon the Brown Bear. Hopefully this book will assist us all in raising more self-sufficient children, the sort of children that our nation needs to remain prosperous, free, and happy.

About the Author

Kyle McGrath has always loved a good story and was inspired by recent events to write one that he hopes both his children and yours will enjoy. A public school teacher from Michigan, Kyle spends his free time fishing, reading and spending time with his family. This is his debut children's book, and he hopes that it will inspire your children to become self-sufficient, independent, freedom-loving patriots.

About the Illustrator

Michaela McGrath is the beautiful wife the author. She is also a public school teacher from Michigan, and spends her spare time exercising, watching television and taking care of her family. This is also her debut children's book.

Questions for Discussion After Reading

Who was the main character of this story? Where did he live?
What did he eat? What sort of character traits did he have?

What was the main challenge that Cannon faced in this story?
What sort of barriers were there to him overcoming this
challenge? How did he overcome the challenge in the end?

What did Cannon learn about himself by the end of the story?

What is the most important point that the author was trying to
make in writing this story?

What was your favorite part? Why?

If you could ask the author of this story any question, what
would you ask him?

Does this book remind you of anything that you have
experienced in your own real life?

Educational Information

This book though was intended for parents to read to their children, and to engage in discussion afterwards.

This book has a score of 83 on the Flesch-Kincaid Reading Ease index.

According to the Flesch-Kincaid Grade Level index, it is written at a 5th grade reading level.

According to the SMOG Grade Level index, it is written at a 5th grade reading level.

But it can probably be read by more advanced 3rd and 4th graders too.

Ordering Information

If you enjoyed *Cannon the Brown Bear* and would like to purchase addtional copies of it as gifts for friends, relatives, colleagues, grandchildren, nieces, nephews, or anyone else:

Buy direct from the printer at:
https://www.createspace.com/4222475

Buy from Amazon.com at:
http://amzn.com/1483966836